This Book Belongs To...
_____

Books by Richard Rosenblum

The Golden Age of Aviation
If Grandma Had Wheels: Jewish Folk Sayings
(Selected by Ruby G. Strauss)
Airplane ABC

MY BLOCK

written and illustrated by
Richard Rosenblum

Atheneum   1988   New York

Atheneum
Macmillan Publishing Company
866 Third Avenue, New York, NY 10022

Type set by V & M Graphics, New York City
Printed and bound by Toppan Printing Company, Inc., Japan
Designed by Richard Rosenblum
Typography by Mary Ahern
First American Edition

Library of Congress Cataloging-in-Publication Data
Rosenblum, Richard.
My Block.
Summary: A young boy living in 1930s Brooklyn thinks
about what he could be when he grows up, such as a fruit
man, coal truck driver, or seltzer man.
[1. Occupations—Fiction. 2. City and town life—
Fiction. 3. Brooklyn (New York, N.Y.)—Fiction]
I. Title
PZ7.R7191765My   1988   [E]   86-28897
ISBN 0-689-31283-0

10 9 8 7 6 5 4 3 2 1

ONE SUMMER AFTERNOON, not too long ago, a kid sat on the front stoop of his house, eating a tomato and lettuce sandwich. He was thinking about what a swell block it was.

He thought he would like to stay on his block forever. But to do that, he had to have a plan for when he grew up.

He started thinking about this, and he got a terrific idea.

When he was older, he would be one of those people who came to his block to work or sell things.

Like Joe, the ice cream man. He had a brown horse and a green wagon. He appeared in the spring and came every day through the summer and early fall.

Joe sold ice cream pops, Dixie cups, Popsicles, and Fudgsicles. For seven cents, you could get an ice cream pop or a small cup of ices.

Sometimes, when you finished your pop, it would say "Lucky Stick" on the part under the ice cream and then you could get one free.

He could be a fruit man!

The fruit man had a horse and wagon too and came all through the year. Everyone called him the fruit man even though he sold vegetables, too.

In the summer the horse wore a straw hat and in cold weather, an old blanket.

Sometimes the fruit man would give his horse a nose bag of food while he took care of his customers.

Each fruit man had his own call.

F–R–E–S–H F–R–U–I–T
or
W–A–T–E–R–M–E–L–O–N–S
or
I GOT PEACHES (or broccoli or oranges)
Each housewife bought her produce from her favorite fruit man.

Maybe he'd become a coal truck driver.

All the houses on the block were heated by coal furnaces in the cellars. Next to each furnace was the coal bin.

Coal was delivered in a big truck by the coal truck driver and his helpers. They were big and strong and wore leather aprons.

They filled barrels with coal and rolled them up to the coal chute stuck in a basement window. They'd empty barrel after barrel down the chute.

It took all morning or afternoon to fill a bin.

There was the "I cash clothes man."

He walked from house to house carrying a sack of clothes over his shoulder.

In each alleyway, he'd yell out, "I cash clothes."

People sold him their old clothes and he put them in his sack. Then he went on up the next alley.

Or even better, he could be a tuba player, in the street band.

The street band went from alleyway to alleyway serenading everyone.

Mothers threw pennies wrapped in paper from their kitchen windows to pay for the concert.

An even better choice would be the junk man.

The junk man had a horse and wagon with cowbells hanging in back of the driver's seat, which jangled to let people know he was coming.

Since he loved to play with the junk in his own basement, the kid thought, he'd probably love to go into other people's basements to buy their junk.

Seltzer is carbonated water in a special bottle with a spigot.

Almost every family ordered a case of seltzer every week. They used it to make wonderful drinks flavored with chocolate or fruit.

He might be a seltzer man, delivering the seltzer cases and bottles of flavors to the back doors and carrying the empty cases back to the big truck.

The trouble with being a milkman, he thought, is that you have to get up very early to deliver the milk for breakfast.

People left notes in their empty bottles telling how much milk or cream they wanted or that they were going on vacation.

The milkman's horse was very smart. He followed from house to house and waited patiently while the milkman delivered each order of milk and cream.

The flower man was Grandma's favorite.

When he came down the block, Grandma came out and they talked about the plants and flowers he sold. Sometimes he and Grandma went to the backyard to look at her garden.

He wouldn't mind being a fireman, but the trouble with a fireman is that he only came to the block when there was a fire.

To grow up and be the candy man and live on his block would surely be the best, he thought.

He'd stand on the corner on the way to the school, just where Pete, the candy man, stood. He'd have the same cart and he'd charge a penny for each candy, just like Pete did.

He'd sell jawbreakers, baseball and war and Indian card gum, licorice sticks, chocolate kisses, Black Crows, candy dots on long sheets of paper, lollipops, bubble gum, jelly beans, wild cherry drops, Goobers, chocolate raisins, Baby Ruths, Indian corn, suckers, red-hots, twists, salty pumpkin seeds, Indian nuts, Charms, caramels, Tootsie Rolls, nut and raisin bars, licorice pipes, root beer barrels, chocolate peanut butter cups, chocolate stars, red licorice buttons, Milky Ways, chocolate covered marsh-mallows, peanut brittle, mint leaves, chocolate cherries, gumdrops, red raspberries, licorice and chocolate cigars, holiday candies (like candy hearts with sayings on them for Valentine's Day), marshmallow bananas, and chocolate-covered vanilla creams. . . . Just like Pete.

The candy man had no bags. Everything you bought went into your pocket or handkerchief.

Becoming an iceman was a definite possibility. Since most of the houses had iceboxes, not refrigerators, the iceman was pretty important.

He carried the big cakes of ice into the house with ice tongs, and on hot days, while he was making a delivery, kids helped themselves to slivers of ice from the back of the truck. His ice truck was beautifully painted with the word *ICE* in big, colorful letters.

The best thing about the scissors grinder was his bell.

He rang this bell by stepping on it. It was very loud and sounded like a school bell. C–L–A–N–G !!

The scissors grinder sharpened knives, and scissors, and fixed umbrellas. He worked inside his truck and all you could see were a lot of sparks.

If he could keep from eating up all the cupcakes, being a bakery man could be a lot of fun.

He came in his truck every morning, wearing a uniform.

And he delivered a tray of fresh cakes and bread to each house.

There was a man who took your picture while you sat on his pony. That seemed like fun.

The man couldn't ride the pony himself, because he was pretty big and the pony was pretty small, so he had to lead it from block to block.

Being a policeman and riding up the block in a patrol car would certainly be a good way to stay on the block.

The trouble with being a policeman, he thought, is that he'd have to break up the stickball or punchball games when older people complained, or find the kid who hadn't meant to break the window.

Then there was the trolley car that passed near his house. Even though it didn't go right to the block, it was pretty close, and he could drive it to swell places and still be near home.

The trolley took families to Coney Island or Prospect Park, and it also took kids and their fathers to Ebbets Field to watch the Dodgers play baseball.

He considered all of these possibilities for a long time.
Then, when he grew up, he became an artist. He still lives
on the same block. He still thinks it's the best block in the city,
and so do his grandchildren!